MISSING

MYSTERY
SIGHTINGS

CA

HUGE
FUR
ORANG
STR
CA
WITH
FU
CA
HU

A
RR
GE
URR
NGE
TRIPE
AT

PEACE
AND
BISCUITS

WE W
MOR
FISH

For Carlier, my Dad.

PAVILION

First published in the UK in 2019 by
Pavilion Books Company Limited
43 Great Ormond Street
London, WC1N 3HZ

Text and illustrations © Emma Lazell 2019

The moral rights of the author and illustrator have
been asserted

Publisher and Editor: Neil Dunnicliffe
Assistant Editor: Harriet Grylls
Art Director: Anna Lubecka

ISBN: 9781843654018

A CIP catalogue record for this book is available from the British
Library.

10 9 8 7 6 5 4 3 2

Reproduction by Mission Productions Ltd., Hong Kong
Printed by GPS Group, Slovenia

This book can be ordered directly from the publisher online at
www.pavilionbooks.com, or try your local bookshop.

MIX
Paper from
responsible sources
FSC
www.fsc.org   FSC® C118234

BIG CAT

Emma Lazell

We were busy searching
in the back garden for
Grandma's missing glasses,

when...

"Grandma look, I've found a cat."

"...Oh aren't you just the **cutest**, prettiest, most **handsome** kitty **cat**," said Grandma.

"...we can't keep you. You must belong to one of the neighbours."

ding-dong

So we went round to
ask the neighbours
whether they had
lost a cat, but...

...they were not cat people,

and, quite frankly, were

fed up of all Grandma's cats pooping on their flower beds and widdling in their garden sheds

Anyway, we kept Big Cat.
He was a bit different
from Grandma's other cats.

Much

more

fun!

Much less grumpy...

...and much more

practical!

Grandma couldn't understand why
we kept running out of cat food.

She texted her supplier, Carl-the-cat-food-man, again!

Come to think of it, human food
seemed to be disappearing too!

Then
one
day
the
doorbell
rang.

Ding
Dong

Hmm I wonder who that could be?

It can't be Carl-the-cat-food-man
because he came this morning,

and it can't be Grandma's new glasses
because they're not due until tomorrow.
Let's go downstairs and see.

"Helloooo," growled the callers, "we were in the neighbourhood looking for our missing son when we found these glasses. Could they be yours?"

Grandma was delighted to have her glasses back, so she
decided to invite the guests in for some tea and cake.

She wondered if there
was any way she could help
them find their missing son.

"Oh my g👀dness!

TIGERS!"

Luckily, **very** friendly tigers.

With impeccable manners.

So now I go to tea with the tigers every week...

...and Grandma has got herself

lots and lots

and lots
of spare specs.

But even with her
new glasses...

...Grandma doesn't notice

everything!